EMM
TALKING RABBIT

Collins
RED
STORYBOOK

EMMA'S TALKING RABBIT

LEON ROSSELSON

ILLUSTRATED BY KATEY FARRELL

Collins

An Imprint of HarperCollins*Publishers*

For Yolanda, who heard these stories first

First published in Great Britain
by Collins in hardback 1996
This edition published in 1999
Collins is an imprint of
HarperCollins*Publishers* Ltd
77–85 Fulham Palace Road,
Hammersmith, London, W6 8JB

1 3 5 7 9 8 6 4 2

Text copyright © Leon Rosselson 1996
Illustrations copyright © Katey Farrell 1996

ISBN 0 00 675206 3

The author and illustrator assert the moral right to be
identified as the author and illustrator of the work.

Printed and bound in Great Britain
by Caledonian International Book Manufacturing Ltd,
Glasgow G64

Contents

One

Emma and the Rabbit

Emma prodded the sausages on her plate with a fork. 'What's in these?' she asked.

'Minced cat,' Andrew answered, quick as a flash. He looked at her and grinned. He loved teasing his sister.

'Andrew!' warned his mother.

'Don't listen to him,' Tom said, giving Emma a slow smile. 'They're really made of—' he paused and raised his forefinger '—crushed spiders and pig's blood,' he yelled triumphantly.

'I hate you,' shouted Emma. 'You're horrible.'

'For goodness sake, stop it!' their mother ordered. 'Leave your sister alone,' she told the boys. And turning to Emma, she said in a strained voice, 'They're vegetarian sausages, Em. There's no meat in them. If you don't want to eat them, don't. But please don't make a fuss.'

Emma pushed the sausages to one side of her plate. She wasn't going to eat them. Maybe the packet said they were vegetarian sausages but she didn't see any reason to believe everything they put on packets. They might be making it up. How could anyone tell? Anyway, she wasn't going to take the chance.

She put a potato in her mouth and chewed. She didn't feel much like eating. She was boiling inside. Her brothers were always making fun of her and her mother wasn't taking her part. She felt as if she'd been told off when it wasn't her fault. Just because she was a vegetarian, just because she wouldn't eat meat, they all thought she was silly. They said it was a 'phase'. She'll grow out if it, they said. But they were wrong. She loved animals and she wasn't

going to eat meat; not now, not ever. So there.

'I expect you'd eat minced cat and squashed spiders. I expect you'd eat disgusting things like that, you would, wouldn't you?' she said, aiming her taunt at her two older brothers.

'Course I would,' Andrew said.

'Minced cat. Yummy.' Tom licked his lips.

Their father put down his knife and fork and looked at his children. 'I'd rather like to eat my dinner in peace,' he said. 'If you don't mind.'

Mr Barnes wasn't given to making long speeches. In fact, he rarely said anything much. Sometimes, whole mealtimes would pass without him uttering one word, except maybe for, 'Pass the salt, please,' or, 'This meat's a bit tough'. So when he did speak, the children knew they'd better listen. They were quite civil to each other for the rest of the meal. Emma hardly ate anything. She seemed to have lost her appetite.

'Fusspot!' Andrew hissed at her as they were clearing the plates from the dinner table.

Their father settled himself into the armchair. He always had a nap on a Sunday afternoon. 'If I didn't have a nap,' he used to explain, 'how would I know it was Sunday?'

'Can we take the football to the park?' Andrew asked his mother.

'It's a bit hot to play football, isn't it?'

'Never!' Tom and Andrew chorused.

'Take Emma with you, then,' she said.

'Oh, Mum! She can't play football.'

'Yes, I can but I'm not going with them,' objected Emma. 'They're disgusting.'

'Help me wash up then,' suggested Mum.

Emma didn't mind helping her mother. In fact, she quite enjoyed it. Anyway, she didn't know what to do with herself. Her best friend,

Charlie, was away at camp so she had nobody to play with.

'I'm bored,' she complained when they'd finished the washing-up. 'I've got nothing to do. I wish Charlie wasn't away.'

Her mother wiped her hands on the tea-towel. 'You should have gone with your brothers,' she said.

Emma ignored the remark. 'If I had a dog,' she said, 'I could take it for a walk.'

'No dogs,' said Mum.

'I wouldn't be bored with a dog,' Emma insisted. 'I love dogs.'

Her mother shook her head.

'Just a little one.'

'No.'

'Why not?'

'Don't keep on, Em. I've told you. I've got three children and a husband to look after. And anyway, you've got a cat. Isn't that enough?'

'Twinkle's all right,' Emma said. 'But it's not the same. She's not my cat. I want a pet of my own.'

'Well, I'm sorry,' her mother insisted, 'but I'm not having a dog in the house.'

'I'll look after it.'

'And what about when you're at school and ballet and visiting your cousins? What about when we're on holiday? Dogs need to be trained and taken for walks and kept clean. This house is crowded enough as it is.'

'It's not fair.' Emma's face wore a sulky expression.

'When you're grown up and have a house of your own, you can have as many dogs as you like,' Mum said. 'Now why don't you find yourself a book to read?'

Emma shook her head. 'Don't want to read.'

'Well, I'm going to put my feet up,' Mum said. 'Don't go making a noise and waking your father up.'

And she was gone, leaving Emma alone. 'I never get anything I want,' she said to herself. 'It's not fair.'

She took a crayon and wrote IT'S NOT FAIR on the refrigerator door and then stomped out of the kitchen into the back garden. It was a very small garden with a brick wall on one side and a wooden fence on the other. Everywhere, weeds and long grass grew

wild. Emma's father said he didn't believe in interfering with nature so he refused to do any gardening. Her mother had tried planting flowers once but they didn't survive the games the children played out there. So, while all the other gardens in the street were neat and tidy with well-kept flower beds, theirs was a jungly mess.

It was hot. Bees floated about in the summer sunshine, settling on the sweet-scented clover and the large white bindweed flowers. A white butterfly zigzagged over her head. White balls of dandelion seed drifted on the breeze. There was a hole in the fence through which she could see Mrs Hardy's garden. Emma admired Mrs Hardy's pink roses. She wished their garden had pink roses like that. Why were all the other gardens so pretty while hers was so messy? Why didn't her father and mother look after their garden like all the other fathers and mothers? Why wasn't she allowed a dog? Why were her brothers always teasing her? Emma was cross with just about everyone.

She picked a dandelion clock from the lawn and blew it hard. One-two-three, all the white seeds sailed away from her. She closed her eyes and wished. 'I wish,' she said aloud, 'I wish I had a pet of my own. That's what I wish. I mean a proper pet,' she added hastily, in case whoever was listening sent her a pet spider. Or a crocodile. She wouldn't know what to do with a crocodile. She didn't really want a hamster either. Her friend Charlie had a hamster and it didn't do anything except run on a wheel all day long. No, she wanted a pet she could be friends with and talk to and do things with. Like a dog.

'A proper pet,' she repeated and opened her eyes. Nothing seemed to have changed. Everything was as sleepy and peaceful and boring as before. A bee buzzed past her ear. She didn't suppose she'd ever get a pet of her own.

After that, she didn't know what to do with herself so she squeezed through the hole in the fence and went over to say hello to Mrs Hardy's black and white rabbit who lived in a large hutch at the back of Mrs Hardy's garden. She wasn't supposed to do that. She was supposed to knock on Mrs Hardy's front door and ask first. But today she was so cross she didn't care about anything.

The rabbit was called Sooty. He was nibbling a bit of lettuce. Emma greeted him. 'Hello,' she said.

The rabbit pricked up his ears and looked at her.

'Are you bored?' Emma went on. 'I am.'

It seemed to her that the rabbit was nodding sympathetically. Emma hoped Mrs Hardy wasn't watching her through her kitchen window. She could be very strict when the children did things she didn't approve of. Andrew and Tom had stopped playing football in their garden because the ball kept going into Mrs Hardy's garden and she'd given them a severe telling off.

Emma unhooked the door of the hutch and squeezed herself in. It was the first time she'd ever done that but she thought she'd be less noticeable that way. She took care to close the door after her. She'd better not let Sooty escape. There was just room to squash herself into one corner while the rabbit carried on nibbling in the other. Nibble, nibble, nibble. That's all rabbits seemed to do. He was eating a carrot now.

'I'm hungry,' Emma said aloud to no one in particular.

'Should have eaten your dinner then, shouldn't you?' the rabbit retorted.

Emma froze, startled. She stared at Sooty, who was still nibbling. She couldn't believe her ears. A talking rabbit? She must have imagined it.

'Did you say that?' she asked timidly.

'Well, there's no one else here that I can see,' the rabbit said.

Emma opened her mouth to answer him but no words would come out. She just looked at him, amazed, with wide eyes and gaping mouth.

'Don't stare,' the rabbit said. 'It's rude.'

'But – but rabbits can't speak,' Emma objected.

The rabbit stopped nibbling and looked at her. 'Oh can't they?' he said sarcastically. 'Well, well.'

'I mean – you've never spoken to me before.'

'You've never come into my house before,' the rabbit pointed out.

'I didn't know rabbits could speak,' Emma said, wonderingly.

'Lots of things you don't know, I dare say,' the rabbit observed as he turned back to the half-eaten carrot.

It was true, Emma thought. There were so many things she didn't know that she didn't think she'd ever have the time to learn them all. But it was, she thought, rather rude of the rabbit to say so.

'I can read,' she said. 'I bet rabbits can't read.'

The rabbit sniffed but said nothing.

'Anyway,' Emma went on, looking meaningfully at another carrot in Sooty's corner of the hutch, 'if you came to visit me in my house, I'd offer you something to eat, I would. It's only polite when visitors come.'

'Now look here,' the rabbit said irritably. 'You come into my house without being invited. You take up my space. You tread on my lettuce. You breathe my air. And now you want to eat my carrots.'

'You don't have to be so bad-tempered about it,' Emma retorted.

'Bad-tempered? Who's being bad-tempered, I'd like to know?'

Emma thought about this. It was true that she had been rather rude coming into the rabbit's home without being asked. And she had been just a bit cross and bad-tempered. She had to admit it because she was a fair-minded girl after all.

'I tell you what,' she said. 'I'll be good if you'll be good. Then we can be friends.'

'Fair enough,' said the rabbit.

Emma made herself more comfortable in her corner of the hutch. The rabbit resumed his meal.

'What's it like being a rabbit?' Emma asked.

'What's it like being a girl?' the rabbit replied.

Emma was just about to point out that it was rude to answer a question with a question but then thought better of it.

'It's all right,' she said. 'Better than being a boy anyway. I've got two brothers and they're always picking on me. And I don't like it when my mum doesn't listen to me, especially when I ask for a dog. And my dad's funny. He doesn't say much. I get lonely sometimes.'

'I get lonely, too,' said the rabbit.

'Do you? I could come and visit you every day if you like. But I'd have to ask Mrs Hardy first. She'd probably kill me if she knew I was here. Do you talk to Mrs Hardy, too?'

'Mrs Hardy never comes into my house,' the rabbit explained. 'But she lets me into her house sometimes. She won't let me chew her furniture, though.'

'I should think not.'

'What's furniture for then?'

'Not to chew,' Emma said.

'She won't let me dig holes in her garden either.'

'You could dig holes in our garden,' Emma told him. 'We've got no flowers or anything so nobody would mind.'

The rabbit shook his head. 'You've got a cat,'

he said. 'He comes round here sometimes, spying and prying and prowling and yowling and making a nuisance of himself.'

'Herself,' corrected Emma. 'I expect she only wants to be friends.'

'I expect she only wants to eat me,' the rabbit said.

There was a silence. It was very hot in the rabbit hutch. Emma was beginning to feel drowsy. She could hear the buzzing of a bee from somewhere in the garden and from further away the hum of a lawnmower.

'Shall I tell you a story?' she asked.

'What sort of story?'

'A rabbit story.'

'Not if it ends up with the rabbit in a stew.'

Emma was shocked. 'Of course not,' she said. 'I wouldn't tell that sort of story.'

'Good,' said the rabbit.

'I don't eat meat,' Emma explained.

'Nor do I,' said the rabbit.

Emma started to tell him about Peter Rabbit and Mr McGregor but her head felt heavy and the words were getting muddled and sticking to her tongue and nothing was making any sense.

The last thing she remembered was the rabbit's beady bright eyes staring at her.

A shadow fell across her face. A voice was calling her. She woke with a start. She had cramp everywhere. She could hardly move. She looked up to see the tall figure of her father staring down at her.

'So this is where you are,' he said.

'I fell asleep,' Emma explained.

'Are you trying to be a rabbit?'

She shook her head.

'Do you know we've been looking for you all afternoon? We were just about to call the police.'

Emma looked at him nervously. He wasn't shouting at her. He didn't seem in the least angry. That was the funny thing about her father. Sometimes he'd be furious about nothing at all. At other times, when she thought he was going to tell her off, he'd laugh and pick her up and throw her in the air. It was confusing.

He opened the door of the hutch, lifted Emma out, shut the door carefully and carried her into Mrs Hardy's kitchen. Mrs Hardy was sitting at the table.

'Found her,' Emma's father announced in a cheery voice. 'She must have crawled through a hole in the fence. She won't do it again though, will she?'

'No,' Emma said in a small voice.

And he carried her out through the front door before Mrs Hardy could think of anything to say.

'Get ready to face the music,' her dad warned her. 'Your mum isn't pleased, I can tell you. She's been worried stiff. I told her there was nothing to worry about but you know what she's like.'

Emma's mother and brothers were standing in the hallway looking anxious.

'Panic's over,' her dad said, carrying her into the sitting room and depositing her on the armchair.

'Where was she?' demanded her mother.

'In Mrs Hardy's garden.'

'But Mrs Hardy said—'

'In the rabbit hutch.'

'*In* the rabbit hutch?' Her mother wagged her finger at Emma angrily. 'What on earth did you think you were doing?'

'I fell asleep,' Emma whispered. Her mouth turned down.

'Don't you dare cry,' her mother said. 'Do you know we've been looking for you everywhere? It's nearly bedtime.'

'I've told her that already,' her father said. 'I've given her a first rate scolding. She won't do it again, will she?'

'No,' said Emma.

'You'd better get yourself ready for bed AT ONCE,' said her mum.

'I'm hungry,' Emma sang in a pleading voice.

'Should have eaten your dinner, shouldn't

you?' said Andrew.

'Should have been here for your tea, shouldn't you?' said Tom.

'Give her some jam butties and throw her into bed,' said Dad.

When Emma was tucked up in bed in her own small bedroom and her mother had read her a story, given her a kiss and made her promise never to hide herself in the rabbit hutch again, the two boys peeped into her room.

'What were you doing in the rabbit hutch?' Andrew asked.

'Talking to the rabbit,' Emma said.

'That's daft,' Andrew said.

Tom did a little dance in the middle of the room. 'She thinks she's St Francis of Assisi,' he sang out.

'Who's Sinfranceasy?' asked Emma.

'St Francis of Assisi,' corrected Tom. 'He used to talk to the birds. Don't you know anything?'

'Course I do. I just didn't hear what you said.'

'Anyway, what were you talking to the rabbit for?' demanded Andrew.

'He's my friend,' Emma said. 'He was talking to me as well.'

They stared at her. 'I don't believe you,' said Tom.

Emma turned over to face the wall. 'That's all you know,' she said. 'And anyway, I'm going to have a pet of my own one day, so there.'

'Says you,' mocked Andrew.

But Emma ignored him. She closed her eyes and imagined herself back again in the house of her new rabbit friend. 'Don't take any notice of them,' the rabbit was saying. 'They don't know anything.' And a smile spread over Emma's face.

Two

Sinfranceasy

The summer days passed. The roses in Mrs Hardy's garden faded and dropped their brown-pink leaves on to the lawn. More and more of the evenings were being eaten away by darkness. Soon it would be time for Emma to go back to school – a new term in a new class. Before that, though, there was something she just had to do. She had to find out everything she could about that saint, the one Tom had mentioned. Sinfranceasy. She didn't want to ask anyone about him, least of all her brother, who'd only make fun of her. She wanted to find out for herself. She went twice to the library but couldn't find any books about him.

One Saturday morning, she mentioned her quest to Sooty. 'Sinfranceasy,' Emma said. 'I mean St Francis of Assisi. Have you heard of him?'

'Oh yes,' the rabbit remarked. 'I remember him well.'

'You knew him?' asked Emma wide-eyed.

'Well, I didn't know him exactly,' the rabbit said. 'Not exactly. But I used to know a rabbit who had a friend who had an uncle whose grandmother's grandmother's great-great-great-great grandfather knew St Francis very well.'

'Really?' Emma said impressed.

'Oh yes,' the rabbit said. 'They used to talk together, St Francis and the rabbit. They used to discuss things.'

'Just like me and you,' said Emma.

'Indeed,' said Sooty.

That afternoon, Emma persuaded her mother to take her to the library again. This time she found a book on saints and hurried home to examine it in her room. Yes, there was a chapter about St Francis in it. 'He loved and cared for all living creatures,' she read. 'And he called them all his brothers and sisters.'

There was a picture of him, too. Emma stared at it, fascinated. He had a sweet little browny-red beard. His hair was cut in a funny way so that she could see the bald dome of his head.

His smile was gentle and glowing. He wore what looked to her like a brown dressing-gown. And he was surrounded by birds and animals gazing at him adoringly. He was talking to them and, she was sure, they were talking to him, too.

Emma sighed. She wished she could grow up to be Sinfranceasy because she loved all living creatures just as he did. Well, maybe she wasn't all that fond of spiders and daddy-long-legs, not yet anyway. But she would probably learn to love them in time. And she'd call them all her brothers and sisters.

She tried to explain this to her friend Charlie on their first day back at school. It was a windy autumn morning and they were huddled in a corner of the playground while children swirled around them, wheeling and squealing and laughing and shouting and kicking things and playing chase.

'What's Sinfranceasy?' Charlie asked.

'St Francis of Assisi,' Emma said carefully. 'I told you. He was a saint. He wore a dressing-gown.'

'What for?'

"Cos he left home without any clothes,' Emma explained. 'So he had to wear his dressing-gown.'

'Why couldn't he buy himself some clothes?'

'He didn't have any money. He gave all his money away.'

Charlie wrinkled up his nose. 'He sounds a bit stupid to me.'

'No, he's not,' Emma said crossly. 'He embraced a life of poverty so he could help the sick and the poor.'

'How could he help the sick and the poor if he didn't have any money?' demanded Charlie, who had a practical turn of mind.

Emma thought hard about this. 'I expect,' she said finally, 'he told them jokes and cheered them up and things like that.'

'I wouldn't mind doing that,' Charlie said. 'I know some good jokes.'

'And he loved all living creatures,' Emma went on.

'I bet he didn't love slugs.'

'Yes, he did,' Emma contradicted. 'He especially loved slugs.'

'Well, I don't,' Charlie said. 'They came into

our tent when we were camping and one morning I got up and put my hand on one and squashed it. It was disgusting.'

'You shouldn't have done that,' Emma said. 'Slugs are our brothers and sisters. You're not supposed to squash your brothers and sisters.'

'I'd like to squash my brother sometimes,' Charlie admitted. 'Except he's bigger than me.'

'My brothers are horrible to me,' Emma said. 'But I wouldn't squash them. Well, I might, a bit,' she went on, warming to the idea. 'I might squash them a bit to stop them teasing me.'

'There's lots of people I'd like to squash,' Charlie said.

'Who?' asked Emma, her curiosity aroused.

'Stevie Dawkins. He's a big bully.'

'Yes,' agreed Emma, forgetting that she was supposed to love all living creatures. 'And Irene Tranter. She's mean. She blew my candles out at my last birthday party.'

'I remember,' sympathized Charlie.

Emma smiled at him. She was glad he was her friend. 'You can come home with me for tea after school, if you like,' she said.

'What'll we do?'

'Play saints,' said Emma.

'Do saints know spells like witches and wizards? Do they know spells to turn people into slugs?'

'I expect so,' Emma said.

'All right,' said Charlie. 'I'll ask my mum.'

'Do you mind?' Charlie's mum asked Mrs Barnes when they came to collect their children after school.

'Not at all,' Emma's mum said. 'It'll be nice for Emma to have someone to play with instead of bothering me. She missed Charlie in the holiday.'

'Behave yourself then,' Charlie's mum told him.

'I'm going to be a saint,' Charlie said.

His mother looked at him and laughed. 'That'll be the day,' she said.

There were egg sandwiches for tea. And cheese and salad sandwiches. And scones and strawberry jam. And raisin cake. Andrew and Tom were still at school playing a practice football match so Emma and Charlie had the table to themselves.

Emma nudged Charlie. 'Don't eat all your

sandwiches,' she whispered.

'Why not?' Charlie whispered back.

'Put some in your pocket.'

'Why?'

'I'll explain later,' Emma hissed.

After tea, Emma took Charlie up to her room. She showed him a handful of half-eaten sandwiches that she'd hidden in the sleeve of her dress.

'What did you get?' she asked.

He took bits of chewed bread out of his pocket. 'What's it for?' he asked.

'The birds.'

'What birds?'

She showed him the picture of St Francis of Assisi. He examined it carefully.

'I can't see any slugs,' he said. 'You said he loved slugs.'

'He loved all living creatures,' Emma insisted. 'I expect the slugs are under the ground so you can't see them. But they're listening to him all right.'

Charlie looked unconvinced.

'Anyway, I think he's lovely,' Emma said. 'And I'm going to be a saint when I grow up.'

'I thought you wanted to be a hairdresser.'

'I changed my mind,' Emma said.

'Good,' said Charlie. ''Cos when you cut my hair off you made me look horrible. And we got into terrible trouble.'

'Well, we won't get into trouble playing saints. Saints are good. Saints are holy.'

Charlie looked doubtful. 'I thought you said saints turned people into slugs.'

'I did not,' Emma said indignantly.

'Yes, you did.'

'No, I didn't. I said they probably could if they wanted to. But I don't think they'd do something like that. It wouldn't be holy.'

Emma loved the word 'holy'. It gave her a warm feeling inside.

Charlie's face fell. He'd been looking forward to turning Stevie Dawkins into a slug. 'Well, what'll we do instead, then?'

'First of all we'll dress up in our saints' dressing-gowns. Then we'll go and talk to the birds and the animals and all the living creatures.'

'What about telling jokes to the sick and the poor?'

'All right,' Emma said. 'We'll do that as well.'

She thrust the bits of bread into the pockets of her dressing-gown and put it on. It was the wrong colour, blue instead of brown, but maybe the birds and animals wouldn't notice.

'I haven't got my dressing-gown,' Charlie pointed out.

'You can borrow my dad's,' Emma said.

She tiptoed out of the room and tiptoed back a few minutes later with a grey stripy dressing-gown. Charlie tried it on.

'It's too big,' he said. 'I'm swimming in it.'

'Roll the sleeves up,' Emma ordered, helping him find where his hands had disappeared to. Then she folded back the bottom of the dressing-gown and tied it up tightly with the cord.

'There,' she said admiringly. 'You look like a proper saint.'

'A proper daftie, more like it,' he said.

They tiptoed down the stairs and out of the front door, Charlie clutching his dressing-gown close to him to make sure he didn't trip over it.

'First, we'll cheer up the sick and the poor,' Emma said.

'How?' asked Charlie.

Emma frowned. 'I know,' she said. 'We'll go and visit Mr Paterson. My mum says he never goes out now so I expect he'd like a bit of cheering up.'

Mr Paterson lived ten doors away on the same side of the street. His unmarried daughter who worked as a dentist's secretary looked after him.

'Let me tell him a joke,' demanded Charlie who was growing tired of being ordered about by Emma. 'I'm good at jokes.'

They rang the bell. No one came to answer the door. They rang again. There was a shuffling sound. The door half-opened and Mr Paterson's balding head poked itself out. He peered at them through red watery eyes.

'She's not in,' he said in a shaky voice.

Charlie cleared his throat and took a deep breath. 'What's yellow and sweet and swings through trees?' he asked the bleary-eyed face peeking round the door.

'Not today, thank you,' quavered Mr Paterson's voice. The balding head withdrew. The door closed firmly.

Charlie stood open-mouthed, baffled. Then putting his mouth to the letter box and pushing it open with his fingers, he yelled, 'Tarzipan!'

They waited, listening, but there was no sound of merry laughter.

'He didn't seem very cheered up,' Charlie said, forlornly.

'I expect he is,' Emma reassured him. 'I expect he is really. I expect he's having a good laugh now.'

'He didn't wait to hear the end of the joke,' Charlie complained.

'Maybe he'd heard it before,' Emma said. 'Anyway, that's enough cheering up of the sick and the poor. Let's go and talk to the animals and birds.'

Charlie's sleeves were unrolling themselves and his hands were disappearing again. The cord was coming loose and allowing the bottom of the dressing-gown to trail on the ground. Mrs Feather from number 74, on her way home with a bag of shopping, smiled at them and said, 'Are you going to a fancy dress party?' The boy delivering the free papers pointed at them, hooted with laughter and nearly swerved his bicycle into a lamppost. Mr Baxter, walking his yappy dog as he always did at this time, stopped when he saw them and, grinning widely, said, 'Let me guess. You're playing ghosts.'

'No, we're not,' Emma said.

Mr Baxter's dog jumped round them, yapping joyfully, before attacking the bottom of Charlie's dressing-gown.

'Stop that, Brother Dog!' ordered Emma.

Mr Baxter cackled with laughter. 'Stop that,

Brother Dog,' he mimicked. 'Would you believe it?'

As the children made their way back to Emma's house, they could still hear the chortles of Mr Baxter and the yappy yaps of his dog.

'Well, we cheered *them* up, all right,' Charlie remarked.

'Look at this dressing-gown,' Emma chided. 'It's all torn and you're getting it filthy.'

'It's not my fault. I told you it was too big.'

Emma helped him roll the sleeves back up and hitched the bottom of it up with the cord. 'Never mind,' she said. 'We can wash it afterwards.'

'We're going to get into trouble again,' Charlie lamented. 'I know we are.'

Emma ignored him. 'We'll throw the bread in the garden and all the brother and sister birds will come and we'll fetch our cat, Sister Twinkle, and Brother Sooty, the rabbit—'

'That's Mrs Hardy's rabbit,' objected Charlie.

'We'll only borrow him,' said Emma. 'He'd be sad if we left him out. He's my friend. He talks to me.'

'Ooh, you fibber!'

'No I'm not. I tell him things and he tells me things.'

'You're making it up.'

'You'll see,' said Emma. She went through the side entrance into the back garden.

'Anyway,' Charlie pursued her, 'what are we supposed to say when we talk to the birds and animals?'

'Things.'

'What sort of things?'

'We'll tell them to be good and lead holy lives.'

'Is that what Sinfranceasy told them?'

'I expect so. It's called preaching,' Emma said, knowingly.

Mr Barnes hadn't yet mended the hole in the fence. It was one of the things he was going to do when he had the time. Emma slipped through the hole and glanced at Mrs Hardy's kitchen window. There was no light in it. Perhaps she was in her front room. Since Emma had been found asleep in the rabbit hutch, she had always been careful to ask Mrs Hardy whenever she wanted to visit Sooty. Sometimes Mrs Hardy said yes and sometimes she said no.

It depended on her mood. So this time, Emma thought, just this once, she wouldn't ask in case Mrs Hardy said no. Anyway, now that she was a saint, it couldn't be wrong to go through the hole in the fence because saints never did anything wrong.

She raced to the back of Mrs Hardy's garden and returned with Sooty under her arm.

'This is my friend, Charlie,' she told the rabbit. 'Say hello.'

The rabbit blinked.

'Say hello to Charlie, Brother Rabbit,' ordered Emma.

The rabbit blinked again and tried to dive into Emma's dressing-gown pocket.

'He didn't say anything.' Charlie was triumphant. 'I knew he wouldn't.'

Emma flushed. 'I expect he's a bit shy,' she said.

She spotted Twinkle lying on a pile of leaves, bathing in the last rays of the fading autumn sunshine.

'You hold Twinkle,' Emma said.

'Sister Twinkle,' corrected Charlie.

'Sister Twinkle,' agreed Emma.

Charlie scooped up Twinkle in his arms and followed Emma to the bottom of the garden. They sat down in a patch of long grass. The cat miaowed a protest at being woken from her cat dreams. Sooty eyed her suspiciously.

Emma and Charlie scattered their bits of bread around them and waited. As the first fat pigeon fluttered down, Twinkle tried to wriggle out of Charlie's arms.

'Hold her tight,' Emma ordered.

'Take me home,' Sooty said in a mournful rabbit voice. 'I don't like crowds.'

'Don't be a spoilsport,' Emma said.

'Who are you calling a spoilsport?' Charlie looked indignant.

'I wasn't talking to you,' Emma explained. 'I was talking to Brother Rabbit.'

'You're daft,' Charlie said.

A second fat pigeon landed on the fence, peered down at the bread, flopped on to the grass and took a piece of bread in its beak. More pigeons followed. Half a dozen sparrows flitted down and began stealing the bread from under the pigeons' beaks.

'Brothers and sisters—' Emma began.

One of the fat pigeons puffed itself up and rushed at a sparrow.

'Don't do that, Brother Pigeon,' Emma said. 'And don't you be greedy, Sister Sparrows.'

'I didn't ask to be brought here,' the rabbit complained.

Twinkle let out a blood-curdling yowl.

'Stop it, all of you!' ordered Emma. 'You've got to lead good and holy lives.'

From the house came the voice of Emma's mum calling, 'Emma! Charlie!'

'Ouch!' yelled Charlie. 'She scratched me.'

The cat leapt from Charlie's arms and hurled herself at the flock of birds. There was a whirring of wings and a flurry of feathers as the birds rose from the grass. Pigeons squawked. The cat yowled. Emma shrieked.

'Help!' moaned the rabbit.

'You wicked cat!' Emma shouted. 'You wicked wicked cat!' For the cat now had the fattest of the pigeons in her mouth. There were feathers everywhere.

'So this is where you are,' said Charlie's mum.

'We thought you were in Emma's room,' said Emma's mum.

The mothers stared at the children.

'What *are* you wearing?' asked Charlie's mum.

'What on earth's going on here?' asked Emma's mum.

Emma burst into tears. 'They won't do what they're told,' she sobbed. 'And Twinkle's killed a pigeon.'

'That girl!' said Emma's mum, shaking her head.

'That boy!' said Charlie's mum, wagging her finger.

Twinkle dropped the pigeon and fled.

'I knew we'd get into trouble,' Charlie said. 'I knew it.'

But they didn't.

'I suppose they meant well,' said Charlie's mum.

'Saints!' exclaimed Emma's mum. 'What next?'

Of course, Emma had to take the rabbit back and apologize (again) to Mrs Hardy and promise (again) not to go to the rabbit hutch without permission. And her mother, pink-faced, promised Mrs Hardy that the hole in the fence would definitely be mended the very next weekend. And Charlie's mum made Charlie apologize for the state of Emma's dad's dressing-gown and offered to pay for it to be washed and repaired.

'That old thing,' said Emma's mum. 'It's going straight in the dustbin. Ted's had it since we were married. I'm sick of the sight of it. I've been trying to get him to buy a new one for years.'

'I know what you mean,' said Charlie's mum smiling. 'Come on, Saint Charlie. We'd better get you home.'

'And we'd better give this poor pigeon a decent burial,' Emma's mum said.

Emma quite enjoyed the funeral. She had a good weep and felt better. Tom and Andrew arrived as they were covering the body with earth.

'What a waste!' groaned Tom. 'We could've baked it for tea.'

'Yes,' said Andrew. 'Pigeon pie. Yum.'

Emma ignored them. 'I expect he's gone to a better place, hasn't he, Mum?'

'I expect so,' said Mum.

'Will you tell Dad about the dressing-gown?' Emma asked anxiously as she was getting ready for bed.

'You know you're not supposed to go into our room and take our things, don't you?' her mum said.

'Yes,' said Emma.

'So you won't do it again, will you?'

'No,' said Emma.

'Well, let's just say I'll tell him it's gone in the dustbin where it belongs. And next week we'll buy him a new one for his birthday, shall we?'

'Oh yes,' said Emma.

'And Emma – I know you love animals—'

'They're my brothers and sisters,' Emma interrupted.

'I know you love animals but they have their own ways. You can't make them do what you want.'

'Sinfranceasy did,' said Emma.

'Well, you're not Sinfranceasy,' said her mum.

'Maybe not,' Emma said to herself. 'But I talk to my rabbit just like he talked to his animal friends. And my rabbit talks to me, too. But it's no use telling them that. They won't believe me.'

Three

The Runaway Rabbit

In the weeks before Christmas, Emma paid regular visits to Sooty. She always had to ask Mrs Hardy's permission now because her father had finally mended the hole in the fence. But Mrs Hardy never refused her. In fact, she seemed to welcome Emma's visits. They would chat together in the kitchen over a drink and a biscuit.

'Do you know what presents you'll be getting for Christmas?' Mrs Hardy asked Emma one Saturday morning.

Emma shook her head. 'I want a dog,' she said. 'But my mum and dad won't buy me one.'

'I had a dog when I was a girl,' Mrs Hardy said. 'A lovely little brown and white terrier. In this very house, it was.'

'Have you always lived here?' asked Emma.

'Always,' said Mrs Hardy. 'I was born here. I grew up here. I lived here after I was married and when I had children. And I expect I'll die here.'

'Did you take your dog for walks?'

'Every day,' Mrs Hardy said. 'Of course, it was all countryside here then. Fields and hedges and lanes. No cars or anything like that. Hardly any houses. Your house wasn't even built then.'

'I wish I lived in the countryside,' Emma sighed. 'Maybe they'd let me have a dog if we lived in the country.'

Mrs Hardy smiled at her. 'I'm sure you'll get your dog one day,' she said. 'Would you like to go and see Sooty?'

'Yes please,' Emma said. And she ran out of the back door and along the garden path to Sooty's hutch. He was nibbling a carrot as usual.

'Hello, Sooty,' Emma greeted him. 'It's going to be Christmas soon.'

The rabbit stopped nibbling and looked at her. 'Is that good news?' he asked suspiciously.

Emma shrugged. 'I don't like Christmas much,' she admitted. 'We never have a proper Christmas tree. We have to decorate an old dead branch. My dad says it's more fun than a Christmas tree but I don't think it is. And my brothers tease me because I have nut roast instead of turkey. I don't eat turkey,' she explained. 'I don't even like to look at it.'

The rabbit's body gave a little shiver. 'Nor do I,' he said.

'And my brothers always get more interesting presents than I do.'

'I never get presents,' the rabbit complained.

'Don't you?' Emma said. 'Shall I buy you a Christmas present? Would you like that?'

'How do I know?' Sooty said. 'I haven't got it yet.'

'You'll like my present,' Emma said. 'You'll love it.'

'What is it?' Sooty asked.

'I'm not telling,' Emma said. 'It's a secret.'

In truth, she didn't know what Sooty's present would be. She spent the next week thinking about it but still couldn't make up her mind. And then, on the following Saturday, she was given some exciting news.

'Mrs Hardy's going to spend Christmas with her daughter in Wales,' Mrs Barnes announced as they were all having breakfast.

'Great,' said Andrew. 'Can we go and live in her house?'

'Don't be silly,' his mother said.

Emma looked up from her raisin bran. 'What about Sooty?' she asked. 'Is he going, too?'

'No,' said Mum. 'Mrs Hardy wants someone to look after him.'

'I will,' said Emma.

'Someone reliable,' said Emma's mum.

'I'm reliable,' said Emma.

'Ho, ho, ho,' scoffed Tom.

'You don't even know what it means,' said Andrew.

'Yes I do,' said Emma.

'What's it mean then?' challenged Andrew.

'Can you children just stop squabbling a minute?' intervened their mother, just in time because, to tell the truth, Emma wasn't quite sure what 'reliable' did mean. 'You'll have to feed him properly,' she continued.

'Yes,' said Emma.
'And give him some exercise in the garden every day.'

'Yes,' said Emma.
'And fresh water.'

'Yes,' said Emma.

'And make sure he doesn't run away.'

'Yes,' said Emma.

'And keep his hutch clean.'

'Yes,' said Emma.

'That means giving him fresh straw and clearing out his droppings.'

'What's droppings?' asked Emma.

'Rabbit droppings,' said Tom.

'You've got some in your breakfast,' said Andrew pointing at the raisins in her cereal and laughing.

Mr Barnes glanced up from his newspaper. 'Do we have to discuss rabbit droppings at the breakfast table?' he said.

'Well, Emma,' said her mother. 'Do you think you can do all that?'

'Oh yes,' said Emma.

'Oh no,' said Tom. 'Do we have to have that mouldy old rabbit in our garden?'

'It's all right,' said Andrew. 'I'll put him in a stew when we run out of food.'

'You do,' said Emma, 'and I'll turn you into a slug.'

That afternoon, Emma went to see Mrs Hardy.

'Come into the kitchen,' Mrs Hardy said. 'I've just been baking some biscuits. I always do that on a Saturday. Have done ever since I can remember. Goodness knows why. There's no one to eat them any more. Unless you'd like one, Emma.'

'Yes, please,' said Emma.

So Emma sat at the kitchen table with a glass of orange juice and a warm biscuit and listened to Mrs Hardy tell her in careful detail how to look after a rabbit.

'Will you remember all that, Emma?' she asked at length.

Emma nodded.

'And will you manage?'

Emma nodded again.

'He needs exercise.'

'I know,' said Emma.

'You can let him in your house if you like,' Mrs Hardy said, 'but you'd better mind out he doesn't chew the furniture.'

'All right,' said Emma.

'And if it gets very cold, ask your father to bring the hutch inside, will you, but only if it's really very cold.'

'Yes,' said Emma.

'He's a tough old rabbit,' Mrs Hardy said, 'and he eats too much but I'm very fond of him.'

'I'm very fond of him, too,' said Emma.

'I've noticed,' Mrs Hardy said.

'He's my friend,' said Emma.

'Well, he's been company to me since Bill died,' Mrs Hardy said. 'Poor old Bill. He used to love those biscuits, Bill did. Perhaps you'd like another one.'

'Yes, please,' said Emma, helping herself to one from the baking tray.

'I'm going to spend Christmas with my

daughter,' Mrs Hardy confided. 'Heaven knows why. We don't get on at all, you know.'

'I don't get on with my brothers much,' Emma said sympathetically.

'Well, that's how it is,' said Mrs Hardy.

There was a long silence. Emma finished her drink and biscuit. Mrs Hardy was staring into the distance, her shawl wrapped round her shoulders. Her face looked sad and old. She seemed to have forgotten Emma.

'Can I see Sooty?' Emma asked timidly.

Mrs Hardy started. 'What? See Sooty? Well, of course. You must. And take him a biscuit.'

'Does he eat biscuits?' asked Emma.

'He eats anything,' Mrs Hardy said. 'He'll eat your furniture if you let him,' she called as Emma went through the kitchen door into the garden.

Emma stood in front of Sooty's hutch and watched him nibble a stick of celery. 'Hello,' she said.

The rabbit continued nibbling.

'Hello, Sooty,' Emma said more loudly.

The rabbit, all his concentration on the celery, ignored her.

Emma, irritated, said, 'You eat too much.'

The rabbit stopped nibbling and, turning his bright eyes on her, said, 'Too much for what?'

'Just too much.'

'Not too much for me,' said the rabbit and started on the celery again.

'I brought you a present,' Emma said, opening the hutch door and putting the biscuit inside.

'A Christmas present?' asked Sooty.

'No, just a present,' Emma said.

'I see,' said the rabbit, still nibbling.

Emma frowned. 'Say thank you then,' she ordered.

'Why?' said the rabbit. 'I might not like it.'

'It's only manners,' Emma explained. 'I always say thank you when I get a present even if I don't like it.'

'Rabbits don't,' said the rabbit. 'Rabbits have got more sense.'

Emma felt herself growing very cross. But she couldn't quarrel with the rabbit. Not when he'd soon be living in her garden.

'You're not very friendly today,' she said.

'She's going away,' the rabbit remarked.

'I know,' said Emma.

'And leaving me behind,' added the rabbit, mournfully.

'I know,' said Emma. 'I'm going to be looking after you over Christmas.'

'What about your wild cat?' the rabbit inquired.

'Twinkle's not a wild cat,' Emma said.

'Tell that to the pigeons,' Sooty said.

'I've scolded her about that,' Emma assured him. 'And she won't do it again, I know she won't.'

'You don't know cats,' said Sooty, finishing off the celery and turning his attention to the biscuit.

'I expect you'll be great friends, you and Twinkle.'

The rabbit ignored this remark, nibbled his way through the biscuit, twitched his nose, waggled his ears and said, 'Thank you.'

'Don't mention it.'

'You just said I should. You just said I should say thank you and now you tell me I shouldn't mention it. There's no pleasing you humans,'

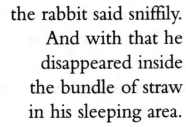 the rabbit said sniffily. And with that he disappeared inside the bundle of straw in his sleeping area.

'Goodbye,' said Emma as she turned to go back home. 'I expect you'll be in a better mood when we collect you next week.'

But he wasn't. When Mrs Hardy had left to stay with her daughter and the hutch had been moved into Emma's garden, the rabbit simply dived under a pile of straw and refused to come out.

'He's moping,' Emma told her mother. 'I've given him carrots and lettuce and fruit and everything and he won't come out.'

'It's your problem,' her mother said. 'You're looking after him. I've got too many things to do for Christmas to worry about a rabbit.'

Emma trailed into the garden again and stood in front of the hutch. She could just see Sooty's nose and the tops of his ears emerging from the straw. 'Would you like to come for a walk in the garden?' she asked.

There was no reply from the rabbit.

'You could come up to my bedroom, if you like.'

Still no reply.

'Please, Sooty. Do come out and talk to me. Don't be sad. Christmas is coming soon. I'll buy you a present.'

There was a snuffling sound from the bed of straw. Emma thought this was a hopeful sign.

'Don't you want a present?' she asked.

Sooty poked his head out. 'Will I have to say thank you?' he asked.

'Not if you don't want to,' Emma replied. 'Only please don't be sad.'

'How would you feel,' the rabbit said, 'if your mum and dad went on holiday and left you behind?'

'I shouldn't like it at all,' she answered truthfully. 'But you must eat. Otherwise you'll waste away and I'll get into trouble because Mrs Hardy will think I haven't been looking after you. Go on. Have a bit of lettuce.'

'Oh, all right then,' grumbled the rabbit and started nibbling a lettuce leaf that Emma had placed near his nest of straw.

Emma breathed a sigh of relief. 'I'll look after you, I will,' she promised. 'Even better than Mrs Hardy.'

Emma was as good as her word. Every day, she gave him the best rabbit food to eat. She cleaned out his hutch and put clean straw in his sleeping area. She let him hop about in the garden and burrow in the earth. She took him into her bedroom and made sure the cat didn't bother him. She kept him well away from Tom and Andrew who were still threatening to put him in a stew. But he still seemed a little sad. So she phoned her friend, Charlie, and explained the problem.

'Can you come over and help me cheer him up?' she asked.

'How do you cheer up a rabbit?' Charlie wanted to know.

'You could tell him one of your jokes,' Emma suggested.

'I don't think rabbits understand jokes,' Charlie said.

'He might. He understands everything I tell him.'

'Says you,' Charlie retorted.

Emma sighed. She knew no one believed her when she said she and the rabbit talked together. And the strange thing was that the rabbit only ever spoke to Emma.

'Do you know any rabbit jokes?' she asked.

'I know lots of elephant jokes,' Charlie said.

'Elephant jokes are good,' Emma said. 'I've got to go Christmas shopping with my mum today. I'm buying presents for everybody. I'm buying a special present for Sooty.'

'What are you going to give him?'

'I don't know yet. Can you come round tomorrow and tell Sooty some elephant jokes?'

'Tomorrow's Sunday,' Charlie said.

'Yes,' said Emma. 'Come after lunch. My dad'll be asleep by then. He always has a nap on Sunday afternoons.'

So the next day, Charlie's stepfather walked him round to Emma's house and Emma's mum promised to bring him back before it was dark.

'We've got a giant Christmas tree,' Charlie informed Emma as they marched into the garden to visit Sooty. 'It's as tall as the ceiling. And it's got lights and decorations and everything.'

'We've got a dead branch again,' Emma sighed. 'It's boring.'

'What did you buy Sooty for Christmas?' asked Charlie.

'A plate,' said Emma. 'But don't tell him 'cos it's a surprise.'

Charlie looked at her and shook his head.

'I bought you a present, too.'

'What is it?' asked Charlie.

'Not telling. You'll have to wait till Christmas Day.'

Sooty was lying flat on some straw with his eyes closed. For once, he wasn't eating.

'Charlie's come to tell you a joke,' said Emma.

The rabbit took no notice.

'It'll cheer you up,' said Emma. 'It's an elephant joke. He doesn't know any rabbit jokes.'

The rabbit's nose twitched. His ears pricked up.

'Go on, Charlie,' urged Emma. 'He's listening. Tell him a joke.'

Charlie shifted uncomfortably from one foot to the other. 'I feel stupid,' he said. 'Telling a rabbit a joke is stupid.'

'Go on, Charlie!'

'OK.' Charlie cleared his throat. 'What's the

difference between a biscuit and an elephant?' he asked the rabbit.

The rabbit sat up and scratched his ear.

'Give up?' Charlie grinned triumphantly. 'You can't dip an elephant in your tea,' he yelled, giving a loud whoop which so startled the rabbit that he ran round and round his hutch.

'There you are,' Emma said. 'He thought that was really funny.'

'How do you know?'

'He's running round and round.'

'Is that what rabbits do when they hear a joke?'

'I expect so,' said Emma. 'I'm going to let him out into the garden and then you can tell him another joke.'

'Won't he run away?' asked Charlie.

'What for?'

'I thought if you let them out they'd run away. Go and live with all the other rabbits.'

Emma shook her head. 'He lives here,' she said. 'He's happy here.'

'Well, I'd run away if I was a rabbit,' Charlie said. 'I'd go and live in a field and play rabbit games all day long, I would.'

'Well, you're not a rabbit,' Emma said severely.

She opened the door of the hutch and lifted Sooty out on to the long, tangled grass. He hopped over to the plum tree and began gnawing the bark. At that moment, Mr Batty poked his head over the garden wall. He lived on the other side of their house from Mrs Hardy. He was always teasing Emma and making jokes which she didn't think were funny. And sometimes she'd heard him arguing with her father and telling him he ought to mow the lawn and clear away the weeds which, he said, were invading his garden. He was a big man with thick lips, a red pudgy face and greased-back hair. Emma didn't like him at all.

'That's a nice fat rabbit you've got there,' Mr Batty said.

Emma flushed. 'It's Mrs Hardy's,' she said. 'I'm looking after him while she's away.'

'He'd make a rather fine pie, don't you think?'

Emma supposed that this was one of Mr Batty's jokes. She stared at her feet and said nothing.

'Christmas dinner,' Mr Batty said suddenly. 'I fancy a juicy rabbit pie for my Christmas dinner. I'm getting tired of turkey. Yes, rabbit pie would suit me just fine.'

Emma felt herself getting hotter and crosser but she didn't dare say anything. Charlie, meanwhile, was staring at the man open-mouthed.

'What are you looking at, young man?' Mr Batty rasped, pointing at Charlie.

'Nothing,' said Charlie and redirected his gaze to the top of the plum tree.

'You just fatten up that rabbit,' Mr Batty told Emma, 'because come Christmas Day, I'll be having him for my dinner. Understood?' Then, grinning toothily, he withdrew into his own garden.

'I hate him,' muttered Emma. 'I hate him, I hate him.'

'So do I,' agreed Charlie. 'He's even worse than Stevie Dawkins.'

Sooty, as if sensing danger, had flattened himself against the earth. Emma picked him up.

'He's trembling,' she said. 'He's frightened.' She hugged him to her. 'It's all right, Sooty. We won't let that nasty man have you for his dinner. Will we, Charlie?'

'No,' said Charlie. 'Do you think he meant it?'

'Don't know,' said Emma. 'He sounded as if he did. He's cross with us anyway. He says our garden is always a mess.'

'What will you do?' asked Charlie. 'Suppose he climbs over the wall at night and steals the rabbit. He could. It'd be dead easy.'

'We've got to do something,' Emma said. 'We've got to think of something.'

There was a long silence while they both tried to think of something.

'Can't you hide him in your room till Christmas is over?' Charlie asked.

Emma shook her head. 'My mum won't let me keep him in my room too long. He chews the carpets and the furniture.'

Sooty was weighing heavy on her arms. She put him down on the ground. Immediately, he started scrabbling at the earth with his forepaws, then kicking away the loose earth with his hindpaws.

'What's he doing?' asked Charlie.

'Digging a hole,' Emma said. 'He likes doing that. He's not allowed to do it in Mrs Hardy's garden.'

They watched fascinated as the rabbit scrabbled with his front paws and kicked with his back paws while the hole grew bigger and bigger. Soon his head disappeared into the hole, then his body, then his tail.

'He's clever, isn't he?' Emma said admiringly. 'He's never dug a hole as big as that before.'

She knelt down and peered into the hole. It was deeper than she'd thought. She couldn't see

Sooty at all.

'Sooty!' she called.

There was no sound from the rabbit.

'Sooty!'

Silence.

'Come back, Sooty!'

But he didn't.

She stood up and said tearfully, 'It's all that horrible Mr Batty's fault. Now Sooty's gone and run away.'

'Do you think he's dug down to Australia?' Charlie asked.

'Don't know,' Emma said.

'Well, anyway, stupid Mr Batty can't have him for Christmas dinner now.'

'But he might not come back,' Emma lamented. 'Then what will Mrs Hardy say? And I bought him a special present for Christmas.'

'I expect he'll come back when he's hungry,' Charlie comforted her.

'I hope so,' Emma said. 'Or I'll turn that Mr Batty into a slug.'

But Sooty didn't come back. Not the next day, nor the day after that, nor the day after that. In the mornings, Emma left food at the entrance to his burrow and by the evening it was gone so she knew he was still under the garden.

The rest of the family were too busy with Christmas preparations to bother about Emma and her rabbit. And they hardly ever went out into the garden in winter so they didn't discover that Sooty had gone missing – until Christmas Eve. Emma's father had come home early from work and they were all sitting in the kitchen munching mince pies.

Suddenly, Andrew said, 'There's a big hole in the garden with bits of carrots and cabbage and stuff all round it.'

And Tom said, 'Yes and the rabbit's not in the hutch.'

Emma's heart stopped.

'Emma,' Mum said. 'Where is he?'

Emma couldn't open her mouth to say anything.

'Have you taken him up to your room again?' Mum asked. 'I've told you not to leave him there.'

Emma shook her head. 'No,' she said. 'He's not in my room.'

Her father looked at her. 'Now, Emma,' he said. 'What's happened?'

So she told them.

Her mother sighed. 'I really don't need this,' she said. 'Why did you let the rabbit make such a deep hole?'

'I didn't know he'd run away,' Emma said. 'It's because he was frightened Mr Batty would eat him for Christmas dinner.'

'I'm sure that was just a joke,' her mother said. 'And I really don't think Sooty could have understood what Mr Batty was saying.'

'He did,' insisted Emma. 'He was frightened.'

'She thinks that rabbit understands everything,' jeered Andrew.

'She thinks that rabbit is a genius,' mocked Tom.

'Come on,' their father said. 'Let's see if we can tempt him out.'

They went into their garden and stood around the rabbit hole. It was already quite dark. The carrots, lettuce and celery Emma had left that morning were still piled by the hole.

'He hasn't eaten anything today,' Emma said miserably.

'Well,' Mrs Barnes said to her husband. 'What do you suggest?'

He scratched his head. 'It's a puzzle, all right,' he said.

'If we had a fox,' Tom said, 'we could send him down the hole to chase the rabbit out.'

'Thank you,' his father said. 'That was very helpful, Tom.'

Andrew fell flat on the ground, put his face to the hole and yelled, 'Sooty! Come out, wherever you are.'

Tom joined him. 'Sooty!' they both yelled. 'Come out this minute!'

'Merry Christmas,' said a voice from the other side of the wall. It was Mr Batty. He had a glass of wine in his hand. 'What's all the noise about?' he asked.

'It's the rabbit,' Emma's father explained. 'He seems to have burrowed his way under the garden and he won't come out.'

'Oh dear,' said Mr Batty, taking a sip of wine.

'Apparently,' her father went on, 'it happened after you threatened to eat him for your Christmas dinner.'

'Oh dear,' Mr Batty said again. And laughed.

Mr Batty's laugh infuriated Emma. 'It's your fault,' she shouted at him. 'He got frightened and dug a hole 'cos you said you'd eat him in a pie and now look what you've done.'

'It was only a joke,' Mr Batty said, taken aback by the ferocity of her accusation.

'Sooty didn't think it was funny,' Emma said, 'and now he's hiding in that hole and he won't come up.'

'Well, I don't see what I can do about that,' Mr Batty said.

'You could tell him you're sorry,' Emma said. 'You could tell him you didn't mean it.'

Mr Batty took another sip of wine. 'You're joking,' he said.

Emma's father strolled over to Mr Batty and spoke in a low voice. 'I know it sounds ridiculous,' he said, 'but if you were to do what the little girl asks, this being the season of goodwill and all that, it might make her feel better even if it didn't do anything for the rabbit.'

Mr Batty looked at him in amazement. 'You think I should send apologies to the rabbit down the rabbit hole?' he said.

'That would be a neighbourly thing to do,' Emma's father said. 'In the circumstances.'

'I see,' said Mr Batty.

He drained the glass of wine and retreated into his house. A minute later they heard a ring at the door. Emma's mum showed Mr Batty through to the garden. He seemed rather unsteady on his feet. He crouched low over the hole and called down it, 'Sooty! Are you receiving me? This is Mr Batty. I'm sorry I said I'd eat you for my Christmas dinner. I didn't mean it. It was a joke.'

He stood up and said to nobody in particular, 'I think I must be mad.'

'Merry Christmas,' Emma's father said.

'Come the spring,' Mr Batty said as he turned to go, 'I hope you'll clear away those weeds.'

'It's a promise,' said Mr Barnes.

'That would be a neighbourly thing to do,' Mr Batty said as he walked uncertainly back to his own house.

They waited by the rabbit hole, hoping that Sooty would poke his nose out, hoping for a miracle. Emma put her face to the hole and said very quietly, almost to herself, 'Please come out, Sooty. I miss you very much and I've bought you a Christmas present.'

They waited. There was a scratching sound. Then there was a scraping sound. Then there was a scuffling sound. A nose emerged from the hole, followed by whiskers, a pair of ears and a whole rabbity body.

'Sooty!' shouted Emma joyfully as she picked him up and hugged him.

'Hurrah!' yelled Tom and Andrew.

'Would you believe it?' Emma's father said.

'Thank goodness for that,' said Mum.

'I told you,' Emma said triumphantly. 'I told you he understood everything.'

'Put him in the hutch and don't let him out again,' her father ordered. 'I really don't want to spend my Christmas chasing after rabbits.'

Charlie and Emma woke very early on Christmas morning. The first present Charlie opened was from Emma. It was a book called *The World's Worst Rabbit Jokes*. Emma didn't open any of her presents. She didn't even look at her Christmas stocking. The first thing she did was to take Sooty's present and run into the garden. She unwrapped it while he watched her. It was a rabbit plate for his food decorated with small black and white rabbits. She put it into his hutch and placed a stick of celery on it. Celery was his favourite.

He sniffed the celery. He examined the plate. He twitched his nose. He waggled his ears. 'Thank you,' he said.

Four

Emma and the Cows

'We're going for a picnic tomorrow,' Emma told Mrs Hardy one afternoon in spring. She often called on Mrs Hardy at teatime on a Saturday. She liked to eat a biscuit or two and exchange news with Mrs Hardy and, of course, have a chat with Sooty. Emma's mother worried that Emma's visits were disturbing Mrs Hardy, who seemed to be growing smaller and frailer, but Mrs Hardy said no, no, she enjoyed them. 'It's nice to have a bit of company from time to time,' she said.

'A picnic,' Mrs Hardy said. 'What a grand idea.'

'Yes,' said Emma. 'My mum says it'll be a fine sunny day so my dad's bringing his umbrella.'

Mrs Hardy smiled. 'Better to be safe than sorry,' she said. 'Are you going somewhere nice?'

'I expect so,' said Emma. 'My dad usually has a map and tells us which way to go. Last time he got us all lost and my mum shouted at him.'

'I used to love going on picnics,' Mrs Hardy said. 'We had some wonderful times, me and Bill, walking all over the Lake District with our knapsacks on our backs. Sometimes it was sunny and sometimes it was rainy and sometimes it even snowed. But, whatever the weather, I used to love it.'

'You could come with us if you like,' Emma said excitedly. 'Do you want to?'

Mrs Hardy shook her head. 'It's very nice of you to ask me,' she said, 'but I can't walk like I used to. Can't walk much at all, if you want to know the truth.'

'Because you're very old?' asked Emma.

'You're as old as you feel,' Mrs Hardy said mysteriously, which didn't seem to answer Emma's question.

'Can I go and tell Sooty about the picnic?' Emma asked. 'I haven't seen him for a whole week.'

Mrs Hardy held up a biscuit. 'Don't forget to take him this,' she said.

Emma took the biscuit, ran into the garden and skipped up to Sooty's hutch. 'Guess what

I've got for you,' she said to the rabbit. He was lying on the hutch floor absolutely motionless staring into the distance. 'Go on,' she said. 'I bet you can't guess.'

He blinked at her. 'Now you've gone and spoilt it,' he said. 'Just when I was getting to the interesting bit.'

Emma was puzzled. 'What interesting bit?'

'My dream,' he said. 'I'd just been made king of the rabbits. I was sitting on top of a grassy hill and all the other rabbits were bringing me presents.'

'What sort of presents?'

'How should I know?' Sooty said reproachfully. 'Hundreds and hundreds of rabbits there were. Thousands of them. Covering the whole hillside. All waiting to give me presents. And then you came and woke me up.'

'Sorry,' Emma said. 'I didn't know. I didn't know rabbits had dreams.'

'Not much else to do but dream, is there?' the rabbit said. 'No one comes to visit me.'

Emma flushed. 'I was busy this week,' she said. The rabbit was really being very

disagreeable today. She didn't know what had got into him. 'Anyway, I'm here now and I've brought you a biscuit.'

'What a surprise!' the rabbit said drily. 'I'd never have guessed it.'

'Don't you want it?'

'Since you've brought it,' Sooty said, 'I might as well eat it.'

Emma deposited the biscuit in the hutch. Then, at last, she told him her exciting news. 'We're going for a picnic tomorrow,' she said.

'Why?' Sooty asked as he nibbled the biscuit.

'We always go for a picnic in spring,' Emma explained. 'I love the spring. Don't you?'

The rabbit wiggled his ears and nodded but Emma went bubbling on.

'It's my favourite time of the year,' she said. 'All the leaves are lovely and green and there's white blossom on our plum tree and I love the daffodils in Mrs Hardy's front garden. Have you seen them? They all nod their yellow heads together in the wind. And you know that purple lilac tree in Mr Batty's garden? Well, some of its branches hang over our garden and if I stand on tiptoe I can just reach high enough to smell the flowers. It's got such a lovely sweet scent. And everything's bursting into life. It makes me want to jump and skip and run so fast I'll be flying on the wind.'

'Very poetic,' the rabbit commented drily as Emma paused for breath. 'And where will this picnic, whatever that may be, take place?'

'Don't you know what a picnic is?' Emma said. 'We take sandwiches and crisps and drinks and things and we walk in the countryside—'

The rabbit pricked up his ears. 'The countryside,' he said. 'Ah.'

'—and when we find a nice place, we sit down and eat our picnic.'

Sooty finished off the last crumb of biscuit and then, looking at her slyly, said, 'I don't suppose I could come with you, could I?'

'I wish you could,' Emma said. 'But I don't think Mum and Dad would allow it. Or Mrs Hardy.'

'That's what I thought,' he said, with a twitch of his nose.

'But I'll tell you all about it when I come back,' Emma assured him.

'If you see any rabbits,' Sooty said, 'give them

a message from King Sooty.'

'What message?' asked Emma.

But the rabbit made no reply. He was staring into the distance in a kind of trance. Emma tiptoed away in case she spoilt his dream again.

Early the next morning, Emma jumped out of bed and looked out of the window. The sky was blue with not even the wisp of a cloud. It was going to be a fine sunny day just as her mother had predicted. By the time she'd washed and run downstairs for breakfast, she found that her mother had already prepared the picnic and packed all the rucksacks.

'I wanted to help make the sandwiches,' Emma said.

'Thank you, Em,' her mother said, 'but I wanted to make an early start. Don't want to waste any of this beautiful day.'

Andrew and Tom grumbled when they were dragged out of bed by their father. They said they'd rather stay behind and play football. They said picnics were boring.

'You've got fifteen minutes to get yourselves ready and have breakfast,' their father announced. 'And no arguments.'

If there was one thing that Emma didn't like, it was having to share the back seat of the car with her brothers when they went on long drives. They would always try to wind her up and, if they could, make her cry. First of all, there was the usual argument about who was going to sit next to the window.

Andrew said, 'It's my turn.'

Tom said, 'I never get to sit by the window.'

Emma said, 'If I don't sit by the window, I'll be sick.'

In the end, their father had to sort it out. He decided to seat them in order of age – Andrew,

the oldest, next to one window, Emma, the youngest, next to the other and Tom in the middle.

'It's not fair,' Tom complained.

'Who told you life was fair, Tom?' his father said, unsympathetically.

Tom tried to get his own back by poking his elbow in Emma's ribs and pinching her whenever he could. Meanwhile, Andrew started telling a story to nobody in particular about a stupid girl he knew who wouldn't eat meat and screamed when she saw a daddy-long-legs until he was told firmly by his parents to stop.

'I wish I had brothers who'd be nice to me,' Emma thought to herself. 'I wish I didn't have brothers at all.'

Eventually, they left the dual carriageway for a narrow country road and drove through a tunnel of overhanging trees until they emerged into the open and saw, on both sides of the road, hills and fields flooded with sunlight. Further along, they turned right into a field which was used as a car park.

'We're here,' announced Mum.

They jumped out of the car and stretched themselves. Emma swung her small rucksack, containing her picnic lunch, on to her back. The boys had slightly larger rucksacks and their parents larger ones still. Mr Barnes hadn't brought his umbrella but he was carrying sweaters and raincoats in his rucksack, just in case. He also had a compass and a map which he studied carefully.

'It's about three miles to the river,' he told them. 'We can stop there and have lunch.'

'Three miles!' groaned Andrew.

'It's cruel, making us walk,' complained Tom.

They set off up a grassy path that led to the

top of a small hill. The boys found sticks and, lagging behind, swished them at everything in sight. Emma danced along, keeping a careful lookout for rabbits. She didn't actually see any, but she did see yellow butterflies and orange and white butterflies and large black birds and small brown birds. And as they neared the top of the hill she heard a flowing, trilling, piping song and, looking up, saw a small dot high in the sky which floated down to earth still singing.

'A skylark,' her mother said, smiling.

'I love skylarks,' Emma sang to herself.

Over the hill they went and down the other side and through a small wood where a sea of bluebells glowed in the sunlight, and across fields and over stiles and up another hill where they sat down to rest and from where they could see a winding river sparkling below them.

'There it is,' said Dad proudly.

'And we didn't get lost once,' said Mum.

'About time,' said Andrew. 'I'm starving.'

'I'm dead,' said Tom. 'You'll have to carry me back to the car.'

Emma said nothing. She felt too happy to talk.

As they approached the river, a small brown and white terrier came running up to them wagging his tail and panting. He followed them as they walked to a clump of trees and stood watching as they spread out the cloth and the picnic lunch in the shade of a beech tree. Emma let him sniff her hand while she scratched his head and patted and petted him.

'Mrs Hardy had a dog just like this when she was my age,' she announced. 'Can I take him home with me?'

'Emma!' her mother warned. 'Don't start.'

'But, Mum, if he doesn't belong to anyone—'

'I'm sure he does,' Mum said firmly.

Emma crouched down and spoke to the dog. 'What's your name? My name's Emma. Have you got a home. Are you lost?'

The dog barked twice and wagged his tail.

'He says his name is Brownie,' Emma informed them.

Andrew pointed at her and grinned. 'She's talking to animals again,' he scoffed.

And Tom added mockingly, 'She thinks animals talk to her.'

'Sit down and eat,' Mum ordered.

She handed round the crisps and the cartons of fruit juice. Emma offered the dog a crisp.

'Dogs don't eat crisps,' Andrew said in a superior voice.

But this dog did. *And* he ate half her cheese sandwich.

'That dog's daft,' Tom said.

'He ought to be chopped up and turned into cat food,' Andrew said.

Emma gave the dog a hug and said, 'Don't take any notice of them. I think you're lovely and I wish you could come home with me but you can't because—' (she glanced at her mother) 'because you can't.'

The dog licked Emma's face.

Her mother frowned. 'I hope he hasn't got fleas,' she said.

'Time for a nap,' her father said. He took a blanket and a small pillow out of his rucksack and made himself comfortable.

'Why not?' Mum said.

The next time Emma looked at them, they were both fast asleep.

'I knew we should have brought a football,' Tom said. 'There's nothing to do on picnics.'

The dog, realizing there was no more food, trotted down to the river's edge and began sniffing around.

'Let's go and see what that dog's found,' Andrew said.

'Yeah,' said Tom. 'Maybe it's buried treasure.'

'A pile of bones, more likely,' Andrew said.

By the time they reached the river, the dog had raced off into the next field.

'Come on, let's follow him,' Andrew said and started off in pursuit.

'Wait for me,' Tom said.

'Brownie!' called Emma. 'Come back.'

They climbed the stile into the next field and ran as fast as they could along the path by the river, Andrew ahead, Tom behind him and Emma struggling along in the rear.

At the end of the field was a gate and in front of the gate was a great herd of cows. The dog was nowhere to be seen. Andrew stopped running.

Tom, catching him up, said, 'Go on. They're only cows.'

Andrew hesitated. 'There are a lot of them,' he said nervously.

Emma ran up to them panting for breath. The cows, flicking their tails and tossing their heads, lumbered towards the three children.

'I don't like this,' said Andrew.

'They're only cows,' Tom said again, but his face paled.

'What if some of them are bulls?' Andrew said.

The cows ambled closer, mooing loudly.

'Let's go back,' Tom said.

But they didn't move. Their boyish pride

wouldn't allow them to be chased away by a herd of cows. Then it was too late. The cows had them hemmed in. Behind them was the river. They were cornered. They were surrounded.

'Help!' croaked Andrew.

The cows seemed angry. Every flick of the tail and toss of the head seemed like a threat. They pushed themselves closer to the children. A few of the cows started smelling their clothes.

'They're going to push us into the river,' Tom

said, his face now as white as a ghost.

To Emma, the beasts looked enormous. At first, she'd watched them, fascinated. She'd never been this close to cows before. But then she became nervous. She saw the fear on her brothers' faces.

'Who are you?' bellowed the cows.

She could smell their cowy smells and feel their hot breath.

She couldn't move.

She couldn't breathe.

She began to tremble.

'They're going to eat us,' squealed Andrew.

Then Emma remembered. 'They're only animals,' she thought to herself. 'I bet Sinfranceasy wouldn't be afraid.'

She took a deep breath and began to talk in a quiet voice. 'It's all right,' she said. 'We're only children. We won't hurt you. We're your friends. We've only come to say hello. My name's Emma and my brothers are Andrew and Tom.'

The cows looked at her with interest. She began to move towards them, talking all the time. 'We only came for a little walk because it's such a lovely day,' she said. 'And now we're going back so please can we pass?'

The cows backed away. Calmly she walked towards them. Two black and white cows moved aside to let her through. She walked between them, Andrew and Tom following her.

'Thank you,' Emma said. 'Goodbye, cows.'

As if at a signal, the cows uttered a chorus of moos, flicked their tails, turned and trotted away to another corner of the field.

The children retraced their steps along the river path. Emma floated along, elated, light-headed. She glanced at her brothers. They seemed strangely subdued. They walked heavily. No one spoke until they reached the field where their parents were sleeping and then Emma couldn't resist saying, 'If you like, I won't tell Mum and Dad what happened. I won't tell anyone you were frightened of a herd of cows.'

'We weren't really frightened,' Andrew said. But he didn't sound very convincing.

They arrived back just as their parents were waking up.

'Sorry,' their mother said, stretching herself. 'I didn't mean to fall asleep. It must be all this fresh air.'

'I hope you children haven't been getting up to any mischief,' their father said, looking meaningfully at their muddy shoes.

'Course not,' Andrew said quickly.

'I suppose we'd better start walking back,' Mum said.

They cleared up the rubbish from the picnic and put everything back in the rucksacks. Then slowly they made their way back up the hill. At the top, they turned to look at the view.

The sun was behind them and low in the sky. The hillside they'd climbed was in shadow. The river winding its way through the fields looked to Emma like a giant serpent. The cows that had once appeared like giant beasts now seemed mere toys.

'We'd better make a move,' Mum said.

And then Emma saw them. Scampering about the hillside below.

'Rabbits!' she yelped.

'Where?' Andrew asked.

'There,' Emma pointed.

'I can't see them,' Andrew said.

'Nor can I,' Tom said.

But they didn't call her stupid or make fun of her.

'She's right,' Mum said. 'They're hard to make out but you can see them when they move.'

'So you can,' her father said. 'Well done, Em!'

'I can see them now,' Andrew said.

'So can I,' said Tom.

'The hill's alive with them,' Mum said. 'Must be a warren.'

'Sooty's kingdom,' Emma whispered to herself.

The walk back to the car was uneventful. Andrew and Tom made no fuss, spoke hardly at all and when they reached the car, there were no arguments.

'I'll sit in the middle,' Andrew said. 'I don't mind.'

Emma put her seat belt on and stared out of the window. It had been a very special day and she'd have so much to tell Sooty when she got home. About the skylark and the butterflies and the dog called Brownie that she'd made friends with. About the cows and how she'd talked to them and rescued Andrew and Tom. And, of course, about all the rabbits on the hillside. Just like in Sooty's dream.

They were soon back on the dual carriageway. All Emma could see out of the window were cars and more cars. She leant back in her seat. Her eyelids felt heavy. Yes, she'd have so much to tell Sooty. She was so glad he was her friend. He was such a funny rabbit even though he was a bit grumpy sometimes. It was a shame he hadn't come with her. But perhaps one day she'd take him to see all those rabbits scampering on the hill. Perhaps one day...

'Emma's asleep,' Andrew said quietly.

Five

Coming Home

It was the first day of the summer holidays and Emma rushed round to tell Sooty the good news.

'School's out,' she announced. 'It's the holidays.'

'You seem pleased,' Sooty observed.

'Yes,' said Emma. 'We're going away this year. We're going to have a proper holiday because we didn't have one last year. Guess where we're going.'

'Do I have to?' the rabbit said.

'America,' cried Emma. 'We're going to America.'

'Ah yes, America,' the rabbit said, nodding knowingly.

'Have you been there?' asked Emma surprised.

'Not exactly,' the rabbit said. 'I haven't exactly been there. But the great-great grandmother of one of my cousins went off to Australia many years ago.' Sooty stared at her with his bright beady eyes and added in hushed tones, 'She was never heard of again.'

'I don't know anything about Australia,' Emma said. 'But I'm really excited about going to America. We'll be flying in an aeroplane, you know.'

'Off you go then,' Sooty said. 'Don't mind me.'

'Will you miss me?' Emma asked.

'I might,' the rabbit replied.

'I'll miss you. But I'll write to you. I'll write lots of postcards and Mrs Hardy can read them out to you. Would you like that?'

'I might,' Sooty said.

Dear Sooty,

Guess what we saw yesterday. I bet you can't. It was – A BLACK BEAR. We're in a place called Oregon in an enormous park and we were walking back to our cabin as it was getting dark along this sort of road in the woods and on the other side of the road a big black bear was walking along. We all stood still as statues and I could hear my heart beating but I wasn't really frightened. I wanted to run across and say hello but Mum and Dad grabbed me and said DON'T YOU DARE. Then the bear went off into the woods. Wasn't that exciting? I think it was anyway but I wish I could have said hello to him.

Love to you and Mrs Hardy,

Emma

XXXXXXXXXXXXXXX

Dear Sooty,

Today we went to a cave by the sea where they've got millions of sea lions. They're really big and fat, sea lions are, but I love them. The best thing is Andrew and Tom are being quite nice to me and letting me do things with them. Andrew did shout at me the other day because I was singing. He said I can't sing (but I can really). So I just shouted COWS at him and he stopped.

I hope you and Mrs Hardy are well and eating properly.

Love,
Emma

XXXXXXXXXXXXXXXXXXXXXXXXXXX

Dear Sooty,

We went for a walk in a redwood forest today. The trees are so tall they nearly touch the sky and so wide it takes weeks to walk round them. Well, nearly. Andrew and Tom moaned and said forests were boring and when were we going to Disneyland. I didn't mind because we saw some deer and little animals called chipmunks. I bet you don't know what chipmunks are. They've got bushy tails like squirrels and stripy backs and stripy faces and they run around very fast like those toys you wind up. I tried talking to them but they didn't seem to understand me. Perhaps they only understand American. They were sweet, though, but not as sweet as you, Sooty. I miss you. And Mrs Hardy.

Love,

Emma

XXXXXXXXXXXXXXXXX

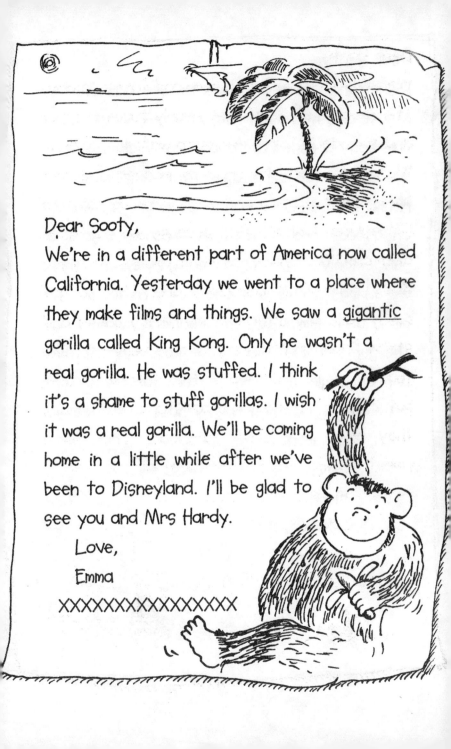

Dear Sooty,

We're in a different part of America now called California. Yesterday we went to a place where they make films and things. We saw a <u>gigantic</u> gorilla called King Kong. Only he wasn't a real gorilla. He was stuffed. I think it's a shame to stuff gorillas. I wish it was a real gorilla. We'll be coming home in a little while after we've been to Disneyland. I'll be glad to see you and Mrs Hardy.

Love,

Emma

XXXXXXXXXXXXXXXXX

Dear Sooty,

Disneyland smells of popcorn. We saw Mickey Mouse only he wasn't really Mickey Mouse, just somebody dressed up to look like Mickey Mouse. We had to queue for ages to go on some of the rides. The best one was a jungle cruise. We got on a boat and it took us through a sort of jungle (only it wasn't a real jungle) and there were birds and animals and jungly noises but the birds and animals weren't real and Andrew said the jungly noises were tape recordings. I think a real jungle would be better, don't you? One more week and then we fly home – so see you soon, Mr Rabbit.

    Love,

    Emma

XXXXXXXXXXX

In the taxi home from the airport, the children argued about which bit of the holiday was the best. Tom said Disneyland was his favourite. Andrew preferred the trip to Universal Studios.

'I liked the forest best,' Emma said. 'And all the animals. Especially the chipmunks.'

'You would,' scoffed Tom.

'Why didn't you bring a chipmunk back with you?' laughed Andrew. 'Then we could have had roast chipmunk for tea.'

'Anyway, I'm not frightened of cows,' Emma said mysteriously. 'Not like some people.'

After that, the boys stopped teasing her.

It was still quite early morning when the taxi drew up outside their house. Emma couldn't wait to see Sooty and Mrs Hardy again. It had been an exciting holiday but she was happy to be home. They took their luggage out of the taxi and Dad paid the taxi driver. It was then they noticed the ambulance outside Mrs Hardy's house.

'I hope nothing's happened,' Mum said.

'She was getting rather frail,' Dad said.

Two ambulance men carrying a stretcher went into Mrs Hardy's house. They emerged a

few minutes later with Mrs Hardy lying on it.

'Wait here,' Emma's father said and went to talk to the ambulance men. When he came back, he said, 'She's had a fall. Broke her hip, poor old thing.'

'Will she be all right? Does she want us to do anything?' Mum asked. 'I'd better go and speak to her.'

'I want to see her,' Emma said. 'I want to speak to her.'

'Better not,' said Dad. 'She's in some pain.'

Just then one of the ambulance men came over to them and said, 'The old lady would like to talk to your little girl, if that's all right.'

Emma needed no second invitation. She ran to the ambulance and was lifted into the back of it where Mrs Hardy was lying. She smiled at Emma. She seemed to Emma smaller and more wrinkled than before.

'I'm a silly old woman, aren't I?' Mrs Hardy said.

Emma shook her head.

Mrs Hardy took Emma's hand in hers. Such a bony wrinkled hand, Emma thought to herself.

'Thank you for all those lovely postcards you

sent,' Mrs Hardy said. 'I read them all out to Sooty and do you know, I think he understood every blessed word I said.'

Emma nodded.

'You love Sooty, don't you?' Mrs Hardy said.

'Yes,' Emma whispered.

'Would you like him?' Mrs Hardy asked. 'Would you like to keep him?'

'You mean while you're in hospital?'

'I mean for always. I don't know how long I'll be gone and even if I do come back I won't be able to look after him properly. Not as well as you can.'

'Why won't you come back?' Emma asked anxiously.

'I'm an old lady,' Mrs Hardy said. 'Who knows what'll happen? So will you look after him? He's yours now.'

Emma nodded.

'Your mum and dad have got a spare key so you can take the hutch into your garden. And keep an eye on my house. Will you?'

'Yes,' said Emma.

Mrs Hardy patted Emma's hand. 'You're a good girl,' she said. 'And you've got a good heart. I won't forget you.'

She let go of Emma's hand and seemed to sink into the stretcher. Emma was lifted down from the ambulance and ran back to her family.

Her mother gave her a hug and said, 'Don't be sad, Emma. I'm sure Mrs Hardy will be well looked after.'

'She said I'm to keep Sooty,' Emma said. 'She's given him to me.'

'Till she comes back?' her mum asked.

'For always,' Emma said. 'She said she might not come back.'

A tear rolled down Emma's cheek.

'I expect she will,' her mother reassured her.

'Course she will,' Tom said.

'Yeah, she's tough as old boots, Mrs Hardy is,' Andrew said.

'We've got to take the hutch into our garden now,' Emma told her father.

'All in good time,' he said. 'Let's get ourselves home first.'

'We'll help you carry the hutch through, won't we, Andrew?' Tom said.

'Sure thing,' said Andrew.

'So, it looks as if there's a new member of the family now,' their mother said as she opened the front door.

Andrew and Tom were as good as their word. They helped Mr Barnes carry the hutch and put it at the back of their garden next to the plum tree. And while the rest of the family were resting after the tiring plane journey, Emma sat herself down in front of the hutch and tried to explain to Sooty what had happened.

'Mrs Hardy's had a little accident,' she said, 'so she's told me I'm to look after you from now on. Won't that be nice? I'll be able to come and

talk to you every day because you're my rabbit now. Aren't you pleased?'

The rabbit said nothing. He just watched her with his ears pricked up and a serious expression on his face.

'Don't worry,' Emma said. 'I'm sure Mrs Hardy'll be back soon.'

She plucked a dandelion clock from the tangle of grass, dandelions, clover and daisies that made up the lawn, and blew hard. One-two-three, all the white seeds sailed away from her. She closed her eyes and wished.

'I wish,' she said, 'I wish Mrs Hardy comes back safely.' She opened her eyes and smiled at Sooty.

'There you are,' she said. 'Everything's going to be all right. It worked last time because I wished for a pet and now I've got you. You're my very own rabbit,' she said. 'And I love you, Sooty.'

'Thank you,' said Sooty.